This
Korky P...
PICTURE B...
BELONGS TO:

_____

_____

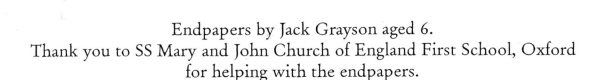

Endpapers by Jack Grayson aged 6.
Thank you to SS Mary and John Church of England First School, Oxford
for helping with the endpapers.

For Zoë – K.P.

OXFORD
UNIVERSITY PRESS

Great Clarendon Street, Oxford OX2 6DP
Oxford University Press is a department of the University of Oxford.
It furthers the University's objective of excellence in research, scholarship,
and education by publishing worldwide in

Oxford New York

Auckland Cape Town Dar es Salaam Hong Kong Karachi
Kuala Lumpur Madrid Melbourne Mexico City Nairobi
New Delhi Shanghai Taipei Toronto

With offices in

Argen   ce
Gua
Sout

O

British Library Cataloguing in Publication Data
Data available

ISBN: 978-0-19-272710-7 (paperback)

Printed in China

Paper used in the production of this book is a natural,
recyclable product made from wood grown in sustainable forests.
The manufacturing process conforms to the environmental
regulations of the country of origin.

www.korkypaul.com

Captain Teachum's Buried Treasure

Written by Peter Carter

OXFORD
UNIVERSITY PRESS

Captain Teachum was a pirate.
He said.
He was the wickedest pirate
in the world—he said.

He attacked castles.

He captured ships.

He burned down whole towns.

And he made people walk the plank—he said.
He was the terror of the seven seas.

He buried his treasure.
He said.
He buried his treasure in ruined castles.

He buried his treasure
on desert islands.

...e buried it in jungles—he said.

He buried it at the South Pole.
He buried it all over the world—he said.

He buried it at the North Pole.

But Captain Teachum had three secrets.
His wife made him do the washing-up!

He had *twenty-five* children!
And he had an awful memory, so . . .

He couldn't remember where he had buried his treasure!
He looked everywhere.
In the ruined castles,
on the desert islands,
in the jungles,
at the North Pole and at the South Pole.
But he couldn't find it anywhere!
So . . .

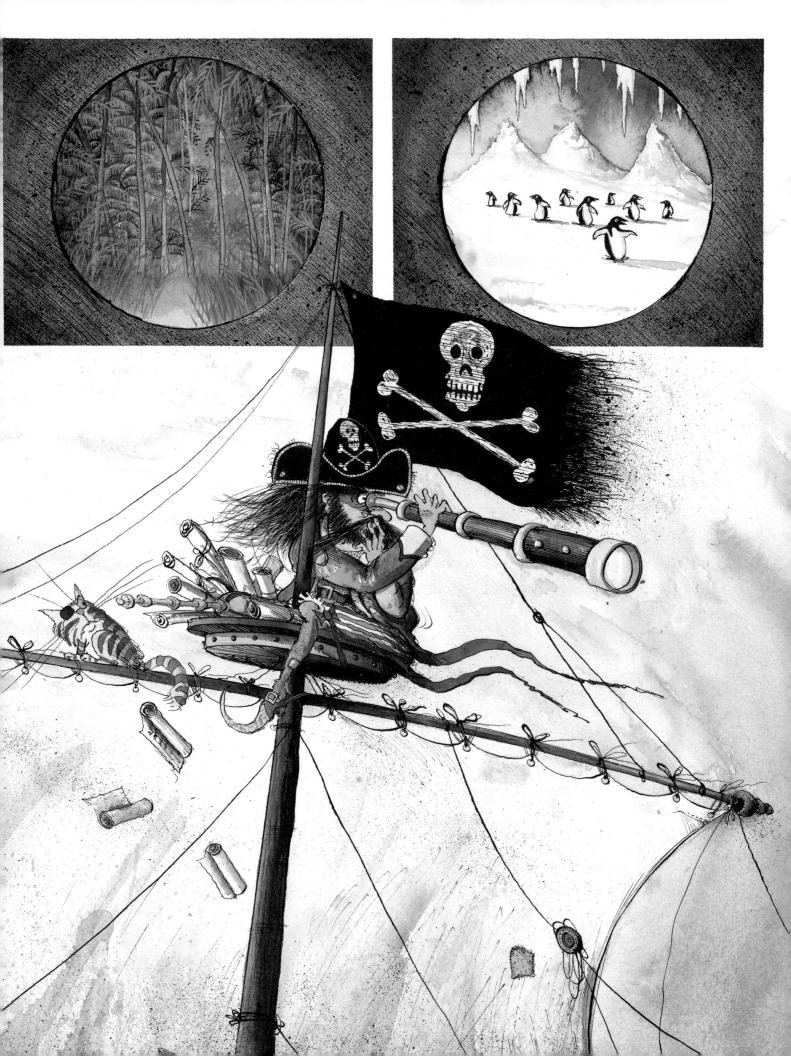

Maybe the treasure is still there.
Maybe . . .
He said.